Lullaby Moons
and a
Silver Spoon

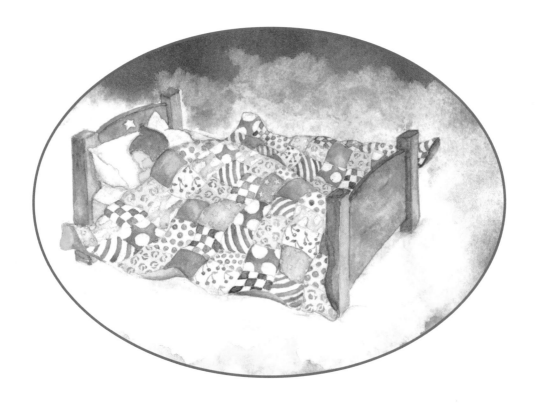

A Book of Bedtime Songs and Rhymes

Illustrated by

Brooke Dyer

LITTLE, BROWN AND COMPANY

New York ❧ An AOL Time Warner Company

For Ayr

Illustrations copyright © 2003 by Brooke Dyer

First Edition

Acknowledgments of permission to reprint previously published material appear on page 32.

Library of Congress Cataloging-in-Publication Data

Lullaby moons and a silver spoon : a book of bedtime songs and rhymes / selected and illustrated by Brooke Dyer. — 1st ed.
    p. cm.
    Summary: A collection of more than twenty lullabies and poems by various authors, including traditional pieces, such as Eugene Field's "Wynken, Blynken and Nod," and new ones, such as Nancy Willard's "Rock Me."
    ISBN 0-316-17474-2
    1. Night—Juvenile poetry. 2. Children's poetry, American. 3. Lullabies, American.
[1. Night—Poetry. 2. American poetry—Collections. 3. Lullabies.] I. Dyer, Brooke.

PS595.N54 L85 2003
811.008'033—dc21   2002022492

10 9 8 7 6 5 4 3 2 1

TWP

Printed in Singapore

The illustrations for this book were done in Windsor Newton watercolors on Arches 140-pound hot-press paper. The text was set in Hoefler, and the display type is Garamouche with Reckleman Script.

Contents

Wynken, Blynken, and Nod

Wynken, Blynken, and Nod one night
Sailed off in a wooden shoe —
Sailed on a river of crystal light,
Into a sea of dew.
"Where are you going and what do you wish?"
The old moon asked the three.
"We have come to fish for the herring-fish
That live in this beautiful sea;
Nets of silver and gold have we,"
Said Wynken, Blynken, and Nod.

The old moon laughed and sang a song,
As they rocked in the wooden shoe,
And the wind that sped them all night long
Ruffled the waves of dew.
The little stars were the herring-fish
That lived in that beautiful sea —
"Now cast your nets wherever you wish —
But never afeared are we";
So cried the stars to the fishermen three:
Wynken, Blynken, and Nod.

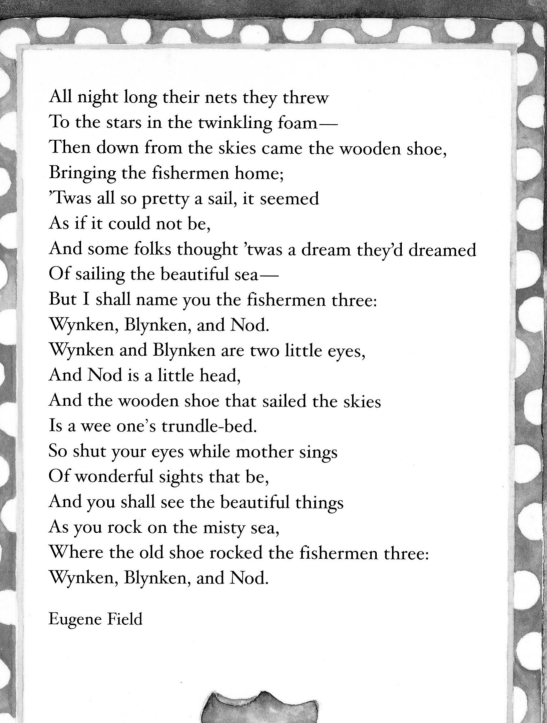

All night long their nets they threw
To the stars in the twinkling foam—
Then down from the skies came the wooden shoe,
Bringing the fishermen home;
'Twas all so pretty a sail, it seemed
As if it could not be,
And some folks thought 'twas a dream they'd dreamed
Of sailing the beautiful sea—
But I shall name you the fishermen three:
Wynken, Blynken, and Nod.
Wynken and Blynken are two little eyes,
And Nod is a little head,
And the wooden shoe that sailed the skies
Is a wee one's trundle-bed.
So shut your eyes while mother sings
Of wonderful sights that be,
And you shall see the beautiful things
As you rock on the misty sea,
Where the old shoe rocked the fishermen three:
Wynken, Blynken, and Nod.

Eugene Field

The Moon's the North Wind's Cooky

The Moon's the North Wind's cooky.
He bites it, day by day,
Until there's but a rim of scraps
That crumble all away.

The South Wind is a baker.
He kneads clouds in his den,
And bakes a crisp new moon *that . . . greedy*
North . . . Wind . . . eats . . . again!

Vachel Lindsay

The Moon

Tonight the color
Of the moon
Is amber tea
In a silver spoon.

Kathryn Maxwell Smith

The Man in the Moon

The Man in the Moon as he sails the sky
Is a very remarkable skipper,
But he made a mistake when he tried to take
A drink of milk from the Dipper.

He dipped right out of the Milky Way
And slowly and carefully filled it;
The Big Bear growled, and the Little Bear howled
And frightened him so that he spilled it!

Anonymous

Mrs. Moon

Mrs. Moon
sitting up in the sky
little old Lady
rock-a-bye
with a ball of fading light
and silvery needles
knitting the night

Roger McGough

You Be Saucer

You be saucer,
I'll be cup,
piggyback, piggyback,
pick me up.

You be tree,
I'll be pears,
carry me, carry me
up the stairs.

You be Good,
I'll be Night,
tuck me in, tuck me in
nice and tight.

Eve Merriam

Lullaby

Porridge in the morning
There's a moocow in my ear
Lullaby and clouds
Cockle doodle don't
Coat and little shoes
Dreaming sea and tea
Anchors away
Once in a while

Sad little moon
Sleep in my teacup
Big Mr. God's
My Butterscotch
Little, yes little
Flea, don't itch
Stars, clouds and bells
And chickens and ships
Always be ready
For beddy-bye

Always be ready
For beddy-bye

Clouds, nighty-night
Stars, beddy-bye
Clocks, nighty-night
Shoes, beddy-bye
Beddy-bye, coat
Nighty-night, moon
Nighty-night
Nighty-night

Dingbat birdy
Do say yes
Don't bang your head on the moon
You must wear your cake
As a hat
Feet, feet, chair, whistles
Clocks and candy
Stars, twinkle through it all

Lutwidge Sedgwick, for the Lullaby Baxter Trio

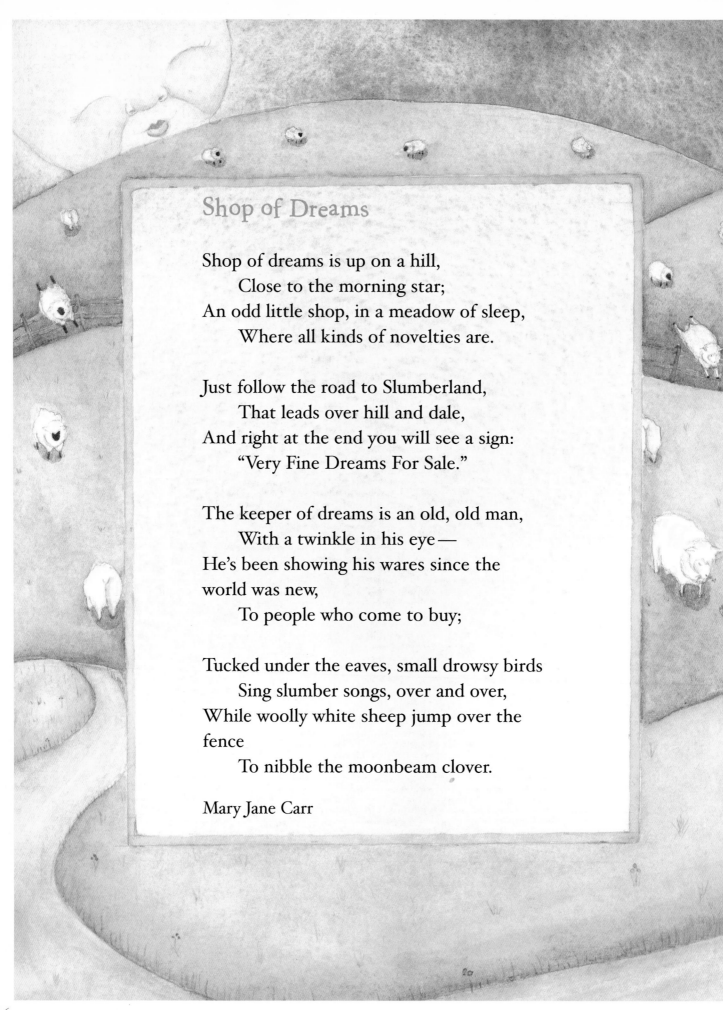

Shop of Dreams

Shop of dreams is up on a hill,
    Close to the morning star;
An odd little shop, in a meadow of sleep,
    Where all kinds of novelties are.

Just follow the road to Slumberland,
    That leads over hill and dale,
And right at the end you will see a sign:
    "Very Fine Dreams For Sale."

The keeper of dreams is an old, old man,
    With a twinkle in his eye—
He's been showing his wares since the
world was new,
    To people who come to buy;

Tucked under the eaves, small drowsy birds
    Sing slumber songs, over and over,
While woolly white sheep jump over the
fence
    To nibble the moonbeam clover.

Mary Jane Carr

Last Night I Dreamed of Chickens

Last night I dreamed of chickens,
there were chickens everywhere,
they were standing on my stomach,
they were nesting in my hair,
they were pecking at my pillow,
they were hopping on my head,
they were ruffling up their feathers
as they raced about my bed.
They were on the chairs and tables,
they were on the chandeliers,
they were roosting in the corners,
they were clucking in my ears,
there were chickens, chickens, chickens
for as far as I could see . . .
when I woke today I noticed
there were eggs on top of me.

Jack Prelutsky

Mooning

What shall we do? O what can we do?
The Man in the Moon has lost his shoe—

We'll search all night on the rubbish-dump
For a star-spangled sneaker or a moon-bright pump.

What shall we do? O what can we do?
Now he's gone and lost his trousers too.

We'll search all night and hope to find
Something that will warm his bare behind.

It's a bit strange and it's a bit sad
But the Man in the Moon has gone quite mad.

He is flinging away all his clothes
And where they'll end up nobody knows.

So don't look at the sky, don't look, it's rude—
The Man in the Moon is completely nude!

Brian Patten

DUMP
THAT A' WAY

Half Moon Cottage

Half Moon Cottage—
A sliver of a place—
Was there this morning,
Tonight it's just a space!

Half Moon Cottage—
One room wide—
Whispered "Hold tight!" to the furniture
And took it for a ride.

Sue Cowling

Midnight's Moon

By midnight's moon
A river ran rune
And a blue-white swan was gliding.
And the silver leaves of a golden tree
Shook as the stars went riding.

John Rice

Little Fish

The crew is asleep
And the ocean's at rest;
I'm singing this song
To the ones I love best.

Hey ho, little fish,
Good night, good night,
Hey ho, little fish, good night.

The anchor's aweigh
And the weather is fine;
The Captain's on deck,
Waltzing in time.

Hey ho, little fish,
Good night, good night,
Hey ho, little fish, good night.

You've been swimming all day,
In the ocean so wide;
Now it's time to rest,
And float with the tide.

Hey ho, little fish,
Good night, good night,
Hey ho, little fish, good night.

Hey ho, little fish,
Good night, good night,
Hey ho, little fish, good night.

Anonymous

The Sandman

The Sandman has the swiftest wings
And shoes that are made of gold,
He calls on you as the first star sings
When the night is not very old.

He carries a tiny silver spoon
And a bucket made of night,
He fills your eyes with bits of moon
And stardust that's shiny and bright.

He takes you on a ship that sails
Through the land of dreams and joys,
And tells you many wondrous tales
Of dragons and magical toys.

So come now and rest your sleepy head
And close your eyes very tight,
For should you stay awake instead
The Sandman won't pass by tonight.

Barbara Taylor Bradford

The Dancing Tiger

Theres a quiet, gentle tiger
In the woods below the hill,
And he dances on his tiptoes,
When the world is dreaming still.
So you only ever hear him
In the silence of the night,
And you only ever see him
When the full moon's shining bright.

One Summer night I saw him first—
Twirling, whirling 'round.
And when I gasped aloud in fright,
He knew that he'd been found.
He turned to me and whispered,
"Please don't tell them that I'm here."
The laughter in his lightning eyes
Swept away my fear.
"If you will keep me secret—
Never tell a soul—
Then you can come and dance with me,
On nights the moon is whole."

So once a month, from then till now,
I've tiptoed to the wood.
We've swirled and swayed among the trees,
As Tiger said we could.
We've skipped in Spring through bluebells,
In Summer circled slow,
We've high-kicked in the Autumn leaves,
And waltzed in Winter snow.

But now that I am eighty-two
My dancing nights are done.
I've chosen you, great-grandchild,
To share my dream, so come
With me into the woods of sleep—
The full moon's shining high—
I'll sit and watch you dancing both
Beneath the starbright sky.

Malachy Doyle

Dream Horses

I am the Dream Horse, black as night,
Climb in my saddle and hold on tight.
Ride with me now to the dark valley deep
That lies at the heart of the Mountains of Sleep.

I am the Dream Horse, fiery-red,
Showering sparks as I shake my head,
Taking you down through the stone caverns cold
Where dragons are sleeping in nests made of gold.

I am the Dream Horse, white as milk
With jewels for eyes and a mane like silk.
I'll carry you safe to the end of the night,
Till you wake in your bed at the dawn's first light.

Andrew Matthews

Burundi Lullaby

A heart to hate you
Is as far away as the moon.
A heart to love you
Is as close as the door.

Anonymous

From "The Bed Book"

O who cares much
If a Bed's big or small
Or lumpy and bumpy—
Who cares at all

As long as its springs
Are bouncy and new.
From a Bounceable Bed
You bounce into the blue

Over the hollyhocks
(Toodle-oo!)
Over the owls'
To-whit-to-whoo,

Over the moon
To Timbuktoo
With springier springs
Than a kangaroo.

You can see if the Big Dipper's
Full of stew,
And you may want to stay
Up a week or two.

Sylvia Plath

One Night

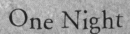

The moon came out of the sea one night
Into a dark blue sky.
It made an enormous yellow light
Across the dark night sky.

The stars came out of the sea one night
And went up across the sky.
They came with a clear and still white light
High in the dark blue sky.
They seemed to be not far away
And not so very high.

Margaret Wise Brown

29

Lullaby, Oh Lullaby!

Lullaby, oh lullaby!
Flowers are closed and lambs are sleeping,
Lullaby, oh lullaby!
Stars are up, the moon is peeping;
Lullaby, oh lullaby!
While the birds are silence keeping,
Lullaby, oh lullaby!
Sleep, my baby, fall a-sleeping,
Lullaby, oh lullaby!

Christina Rossetti

Rock Me

Rock me in a mixing bowl,
rock me in a wing.
Rock me in the alphabet
and let the letters sing.

Rock me in an envelope
printed all with sheep.
Stamp it with your biggest hug
and send me off to sleep.

Nancy Willard

Acknowledgments

LULLABY BAXTER: "Lullaby," by Lullaby Baxter and Lutwidge Sedgwick. Copyright © 2000 by Workin' Girl Music, Mop & Bucket Music (BMI). Reprinted by permission.

BARBARA TAYLOR BRADFORD: "The Sandman," copyright © 1972 by Barbara Taylor Bradford, from A GARLAND OF CHILDREN'S VERSE, by Barbara Taylor Bradford, published by Lion Books. Reprinted by permission of Janklow and Nesbit.

MARGARET WISE BROWN: "One Night," by Margaret Wise Brown. Copyright © by Margaret Wise Brown. Reprinted by permission of the author.

SUE COWLING: "Half Moon Cottage," copyright © by Sue Cowling, from GOOD NIGHT, SLEEP TIGHT, compiled by Ivan and Mal Jones, published by Scholastic UK. Reprinted by permission of the author.

MALACHY DOYLE: "The Dancing Tiger," copyright © by Malachy Doyle. From GOOD NIGHT, SLEEP TIGHT, compiled by Ivan and Mal Jones, published by Scholastic UK. Reprinted by permission of the author.

VACHEL LINDSAY: "The Moon's the North Wind's Cooky," from THE COLLECTED POEMS OF VACHEL LINDSAY, revised edition, by Vachel Lindsay. Copyright © 1925 by Macmillan Publishing Co., Inc.; copyright renewed © 1953 by Elizabeth C. Lindsay. Reprinted by permission of Scribner, an imprint of Simon & Schuster Adult Publishing Group.

ROGER MCGOUGH: "Mrs. Moon," by Roger McGough. Copyright © by Roger McGough. Reprinted by permission of Peters, Fraser & Dunlop on behalf of Roger McGough.

ANDREW MATTHEWS: "Dream Horses," by Andrew Matthews. Reprinted by permission of Peters, Fraser & Dunlop on behalf of Andrew Matthews.

EVE MERRIAM: "You Be Saucer," by Eve Merriam, from YOU BE GOOD AND I'LL BE NIGHT, by Eve Merriam. Copyright © 1988 by Eve Merriam. Reprinted by permission of Marian Reiner.

BRIAN PATTEN: "Mooning," copyright © 1990 by Brian Patten, from THAWING FROZEN FROGS, published by Viking Children's Books and Puffin.

SYLVIA PLATH: "The Bed Book," by Sylvia Plath. Copyright © 1976 by Ted Hughes. Reprinted by permission of HarperCollins Publishers.

JACK PRELUTSKY: "Last Night I Dreamed of Chickens," by Jack Prelutsky. Copyright © 1990 by Jack Prelutsky. Reprinted by permission of HarperCollins Publishers.

JOHN RICE: "Midnight's Moon," copyright © by John Rice, from GOOD NIGHT, SLEEP TIGHT, compiled by Ivan and Mal Jones, published by Scholastic UK. Reprinted by permission of the author.

NANCY WILLARD: "Rock Me," by Nancy Willard. Copyright © 2003 by Nancy Willard. Printed by permission of the author.